This Walker book
belongs to:

by **Katrina Germein**

illustrated by

Tom Jellett

WALKER BOOKS
AND SUBSIDIARIES
LONDON · BOSTON · SYDNEY · AUCKLAND

My mum says the STRANGEST things

When I'm excited,
Mum says I have

ants in

my pants.

She says, "Stop running around like a headless chook. You're driving me round the bend."

My mum says the strangest things.

When I'm noisy, Mum says she can't hear herself think.

When I'm grumpy, Mum says you could land an aeroplane on my bottom lip.

My mum says the **strangest** things.

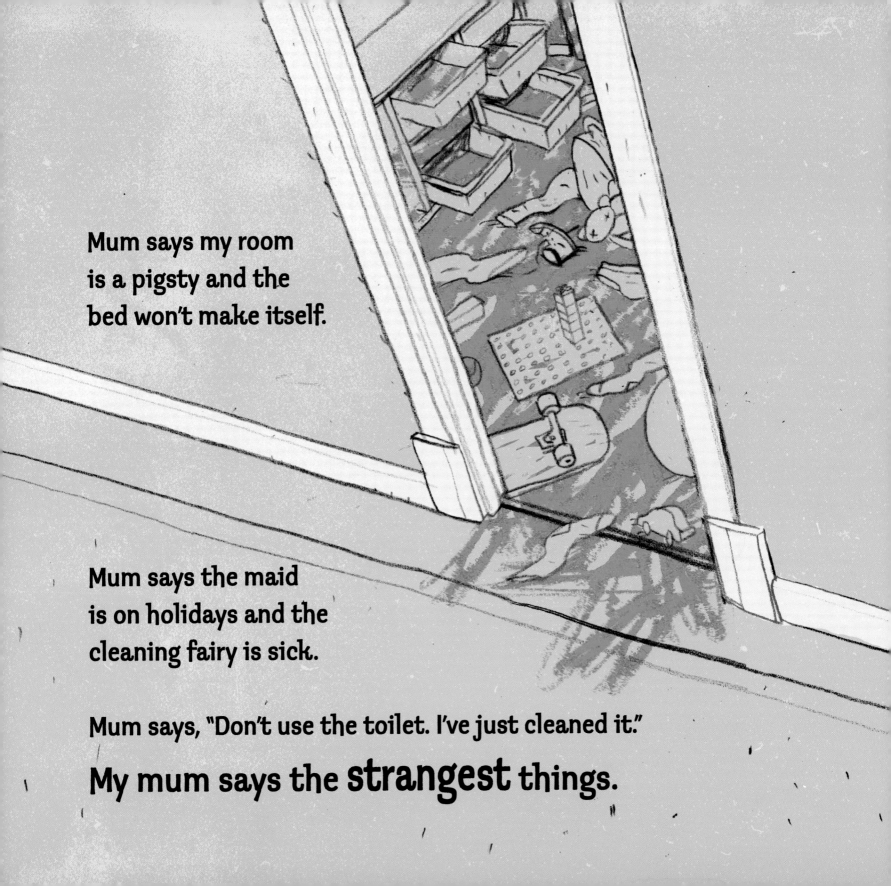

Mum says my room
is a pigsty and the
bed won't make itself.

Mum says the maid
is on holidays and the
cleaning fairy is sick.

Mum says, "Don't use the toilet. I've just cleaned it."

My mum says the **strangest** things.

My mum says that
if the wind changes,
my face will stay
just like this.

My mum says if I watch too much television, I'll get square eyes. My mum says that she has eyes in the back of her head.

My mum

says the

strangest

things.

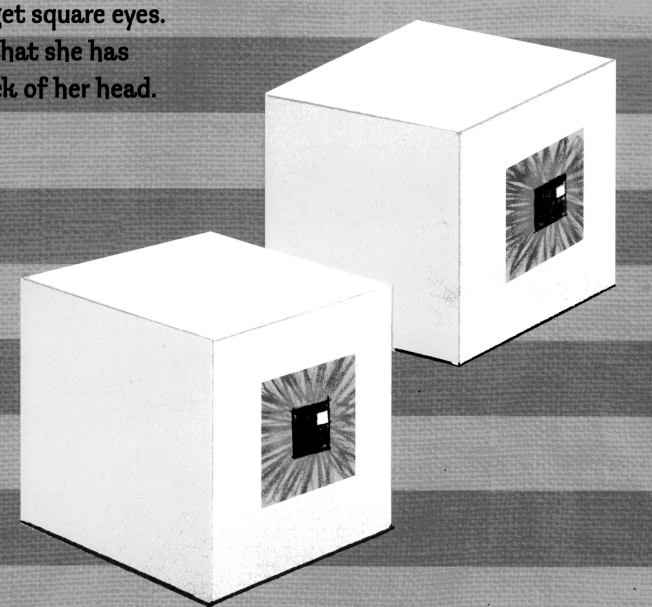

Mum says

spinach makes you strong.

Mum says

carrots make

you see in the dark.

Mum says

fish makes you smart.

**My mum says the
strangest things.**

Mum also says, when her ship comes in,
she's giving up cooking — forever.

My mum says the **strangest** things.

Sometimes Mum says
I'm a little monster.

Sometimes Mum says
I'm a perfect angel.

Cross Mum uses my full name.

Cross Mum says,
"Two wrongs don't make
a right, young man."

Cross Mum tells
me to pull up my
socks, even
when I'm not
wearing any.

My mum says the strangest things.

When Mum's **cold**
she tells
me
to wear
a jumper.

When Mum's **hot**
she tells
me
to sit
still.

When Mum's tired she says **everyone** needs an early night.

My mum says the **strangest** things.

Mum tells me I'm good as gold.

Mum tells me I'm still her baby.

Mum tells me I'm snug as a bug.

But every night when she tucks me in,
my mum says that she loves me,
all the way to the stars and back.

My mum
says the
very best
things.

For the mums:
Sue, Liz and
Doris.
Love you. xxx

KG

For Jo.

TJ

First published 2014 by 🐕 **black dog books**
This edition published 2015
by Walker Books Ltd
87 Vauxhall Walk, London SE11 5HJ

10 9 8 7 6 5 4 3 2 1

Text © 2014 Katrina Germein
Illustrations ©2014 Tom Jellett

This book has been typeset in Klepto

Printed in China

British Library Cataloguing in Publication Data:
a catalogue record for this book is available
from the British Library

iSBN 978-1-4063-5891-9

www.walker.co.uk

Katrina Germein is an award-winning picture-book author whose other titles include *My Dad Thinks He's Funny* and *My Dad Still Thinks He's Funny*. Katrina, who works part-time as a teacher, lives in Adelaide, Australia, with her husband, their three children and an energetic dog named Mango.

Tom Jellett is an illustrator whose work has appeared in a number of books — including *My Dad Thinks He's Funny* and *My Dad Still Thinks He's Funny* — as well as in national newspapers such as *The Australian* and the *Daily Telegraph*. Tom lives in Sydney, Australia.

Look out for:

978-1-4063-4730-2

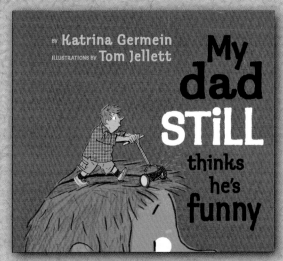

978-1-4063-6055-4

Available from all good booksellers

www.walker.co.uk